minions

Snow Day

By Brandon T. Snider

Illustrated by Ed Miller

Based on the Motion Picture Screenplay
Written by Brian Lynch

These little guys are Minions.
Kevin is the thinker. He's protective of his pals.
Stuart dreams of becoming a rock star.
And Bob has a curious spirit!

It's way too cold to go outside. The Minions will become ice cubes in an instant! Better to stay in their cave and wait for the chilly winter to pass.

Being inside for too long has made Kevin, Stuart and Bob go a little crazy. Hopefully a new master will come along soon and save them from their boredom. In the meantime, they've got one another and that's pretty cool. Friends are the best!

Kevin feels a drop of water on his head. That means the sun is out! Its heat is warming up the cave and causing the ice to melt. Soon the Minions will be able to go outside without freezing their goggles off.

Just imagine all the fun things they'll be able to do once they're outside!

It's time to change out their snow gear. Stuart and Bob could use a little help choosing the right clothes to wear! Don't worry. Kevin knows what to do. Bundle up warm and tight, Minions. It's still cold out there.

Now that the Minions are properly
suited up, it's time for the final touch.
A stick? Nope.
A rake? Not quite. Sorry, Bob!
A shovel? *DING, DING, DING!*
We have a winner!

Watch out, winter! Here come the Minions!

Now it's time to push that big boulder aside so they can leave the cave and enjoy the warm day. This isn't going to be easy.

Oh no! The Minions successfully move the boulder, but the cave entrance is blocked by snow. They'll have to dig their way through. It's a good thing they're prepared.

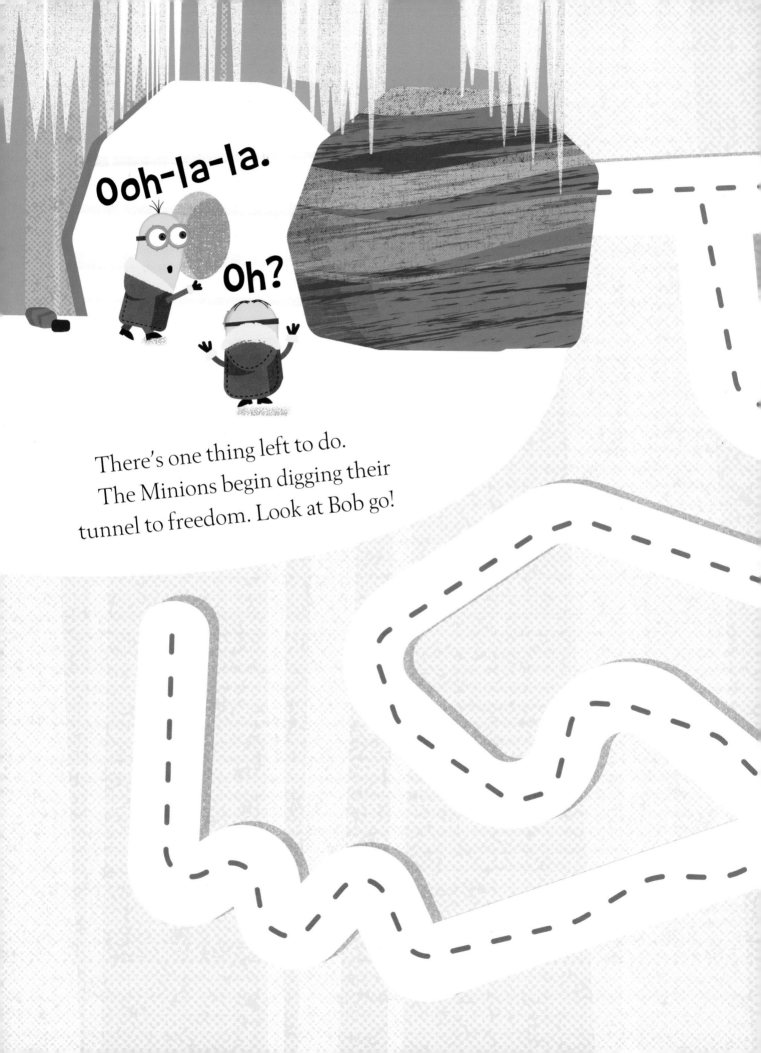

There's one thing left to do. The Minions begin digging their tunnel to freedom. Look at Bob go!

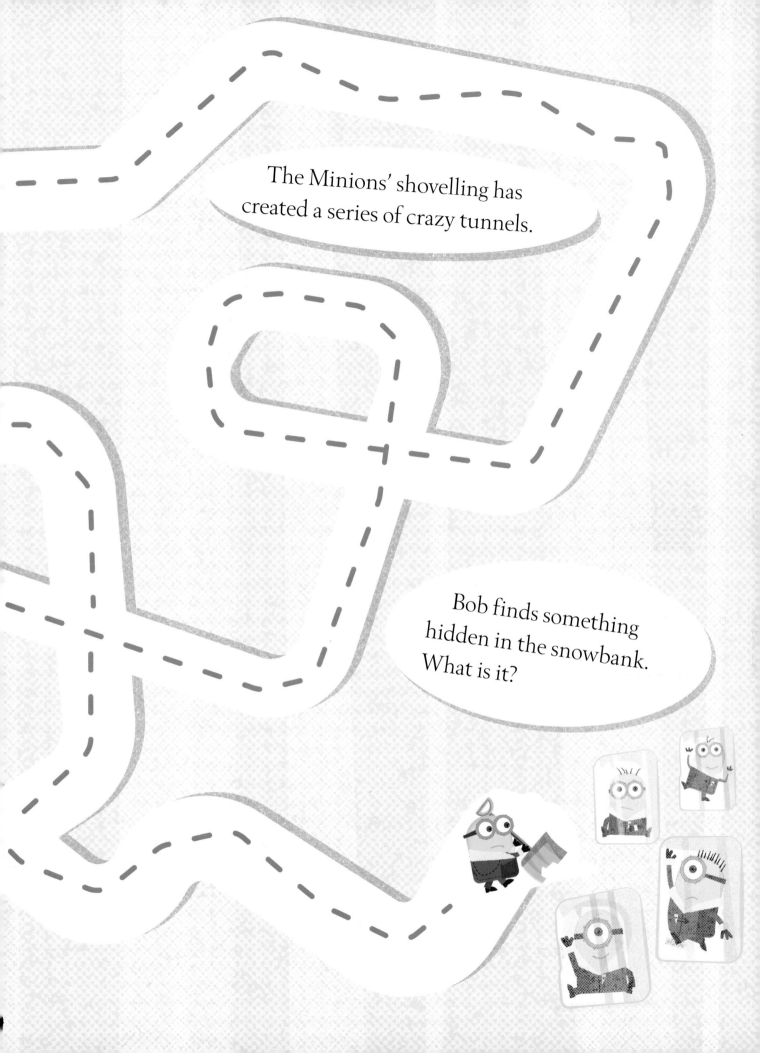

The Minions' shovelling has created a series of crazy tunnels.

Bob finds something hidden in the snowbank. What is it?

Bob discovers a bunch of his Minion buddies and they're frozen solid! Don't panic, Bob knows the right thing to do! Kind of . . . Kevin and Stuart have their own ideas of how to help, just in case.

Once their friends have defrosted, Kevin, Stuart and Bob welcome their old pals with open arms.

Yikes! Bob finds a polar bear trapped in the ice. Be careful, Minion. This discovery could mean trouble!

Ha-ha! Poochie!

Now that the Minions have dug themselves out of their icy home, they're ready to play. What should they do with all this extra snow? Hmmm . . .

Building an igloo is a difficult job. Thankfully, the Minions know how to work together.

Keep going, Stuart! Don't give up!

Be careful, Bob. Ice can be slippery.

Norbert, don't eat the ice!

Dave, Paul, Henry, Brian and the other Minions follow Kevin's lead. He knows what to do.

The igloo is finally done! With pride, the Minions gather around their beautiful new creation. Not bad, huh?
Hey! What's Bob doing?

Oooh!

While the Minions were working, the ice holding the polar bear melted. *Whoops!* Now he's looking for his next meal. Isn't he?

The good news: The igloo is amazing.

The bad news: The polar bear agrees. Now the bear has made the Minions' wonderful ice fortress his home. He still looks hungry, so the Minions retreat to their ice cave.

Bob and Stuart think about how they
can remove the polar bear from their igloo.
They gather the other Minions and show
them their crazy ideas.

Snowman!

WHOOSH!

Luckily, Kevin always
has a plan!

Hmmm.

Kevin rallies his friends
to take back the igloo.
MINIONS ATTACK!

They've got their enemy on the run. VICTORY!
Or so they think . . . The Minions don't see a giant
shadow behind them. Whatever it is has scared the bear
away with just one look.

Now that there isn't any danger, the Minions can finally play in peace.

Bob makes a gigantic snow cone. Yummy!

Norbert creates his very own snow-Minion. Impressive!

Stuart is making snow angels. *Awww,* so cute!

What a great day!

While the others play, Kevin sees the real hero that saved them from the bear. But is it a friend or a foe?

Or maybe, just maybe . . . it's . . .

Big...boss?

. . . a brand-new master! Kevin really hopes it is. After all, the Minions deserve only the best.